Dear Parents,

Welcome to the Scholastic Reader series. We have taken over 80 years of experience with teachers, parents, and children and put it into a program that is designed to match your child's interests and skills.

Level 1—Short sentences and stories made up of words kids can sound out using their phonics skills and words that are important to remember.

Level 2—Longer sentences and stories with words kids need to know and new "big" words that they will want to know.

Level 3—From sentences to paragraphs to longer stories, these books have large "chunks" of texts and are made up of a rich vocabulary.

Level 4—First chapter books with more words and fewer pictures.

It is important that children learn to read well enough to succeed in school and beyond. Here are ideas for reading this book with your child:

- Look at the book together. Encourage your child to read the title and make a prediction about the story.
- Read the book together. Encourage your child to sound out words when appropriate. When your child struggles, you can help by providing the word.
- Encourage your child to retell the story. This is a great way to check for comprehension.
- Have your child take the fluency test on the last page to check progress.

Scholastic Readers are designed to support your child's efforts to learn how to read at every age and every stage. Enjoy helping your child learn to read and love to read.

        —Francie Alexander
        Chief Education Officer
        Scholastic Education

FLUFFY

ON THE GO!

by Kate McMullan
Illustrated by Mavis Smith

Cartwheel
·B·O·O·K·S· ®

SCHOLASTIC INC.

New York   Toronto   London   Auckland
Sydney   Mexico City   New Delhi   Hong Kong

Fluffy's School Bus Adventure, ISBN 0-439-20671-5, Text copyright © 2000 by Kate McMullan. Illustrations copyright © 2000 by Mavis Smith. Activities copyright © 2003 Scholastic Inc.

Fluffy Goes to Washington, ISBN 0-439-31943-9, Text copyright © 2002 by Kate McMullan. Illustrations copyright © 2002 by Mavis Smith.

Fluffy Learns to Swim, ISBN 0-439-31946-3, Text copyright © 2002 by Kate McMullan. Illustrations copyright © 2002 by Mavis Smith.

12 11 10 9 8 7 6 5 4 3 2 1   10 11/0 1 2

Printed in Singapore   46

This edition created exclusively for Barnes & Noble, Inc.

2010 Barnes & Noble Books

ISBN 978-1-4351-2427-1

First printing, March 2010

Contents

FLUFFY'S
SCHOOL BUS ADVENTURE

FLUFFY'S
SCHOOL BUS ADVENTURE

by **Kate McMullan**
Illustrated by **Mavis Smith**

The Big Mistake

It was Friday afternoon.
"Good-bye!" Ms. Day called
to her students.

Ms. Day was about to go home, too.
But then she saw Fluffy.
"Fluffy!" said Ms. Day.
"Why are YOU still here?"

"Jasmine was supposed
to take you home," Ms. Day said.
"I guess she forgot."
Forgot? thought Fluffy.
**How could anybody
forget ME?**

"Maybe I can catch her,"
said Ms. Day.
She picked up Fluffy's cage and ran outside.
She hurried over to a school bus.
"Does Jasmine ride this bus?"
she asked the driver.
The driver nodded.

Ms. Day held up the cage.
"She forgot something."
That would be me,
thought Fluffy.

The driver took Fluffy's cage.
She put it on an empty seat.
"I will surprise Jasmine
when she gets off the bus," she said.
She started the bus and drove off.

A girl sat next to Fluffy.

She took him out of his cage.

"Have a lollipop, little pig," she said.

A what-a-pop? thought Fluffy.

He licked it.

The thing tasted yummy.

But it made his fur green and sticky.

"This is my stop,"
the girl said.
She gave Fluffy
to the boys behind her.
"Bye, little pig."

The boys were playing
with purple goo.
"Have some goo, little pig,"
they said.
They showed Fluffy
how to squish the goo
through his paws.
It turned his paws purple.
Oooooh! thought Fluffy.
The goo felt like cold jelly.

The boys put the goo back into a jar.
They gave Fluffy to the girl
behind them.

"'Bye, little pig," they said.
Fluffy and the girl
were the last ones on the bus.

The girl put her sunglasses on Fluffy.
She put glitter on him.
"You look like a rock star!" she said.
That's me! thought Fluffy.

The girl held Fluffy up to the window.
Some kids in another bus saw him.
They waved.
Rock Star Fluffy waved to his fans.

The bus stopped again.
The girl took the sunglasses
off Fluffy.
She carried him
to the front of the school bus
and gave him to the driver.
"Wait," said the driver.
"Ms. Day asked me
to give the pig to you, Jasmine."

"I'm not in Ms. Day's class,"
said the girl.
"That's Jasmine P.
I'm Jasmine M."
And she got off the bus.

Fluffy looked at the bus driver.
The bus driver looked at Fluffy.
Uh-oh, they both thought.
There has been a BIG mistake!

Fluffy Helps Out

"I know where Jasmine P. lives,"
the bus driver told Fluffy.
"I will take you to her house."
She put Fluffy into her pocket.
She drove off.
Make way for the bus!
thought Fluffy.

The driver stopped at a red light.
All of a sudden,
the bus went *CA-LUNK!*
The engine stopped.
Uh-oh, thought Fluffy and
the driver.

The bus driver called a tow truck.
The tow truck driver put a big hook
on the bumper of the school bus.
The tow truck picked up
the front end of the bus.
Now THAT is strong,
thought Fluffy.

The bus driver and Fluffy got
into the tow truck.
Make way for the tow truck,
thought Fluffy.

They stopped at a garage.

"What is the trouble?" asked the mechanic.

"The engine went *CA-LUNK!* and stopped,"
the bus driver said.

The mechanic opened the hood.

He bent over the engine.

He opened caps.

He poked around.

He tried to start the bus.

Nothing happened.

"Are you sure it went *CA-LUNK?*"
he asked. "Or did it go *CLANK?*
Or maybe *CLINK?*"
asked the mechanic.

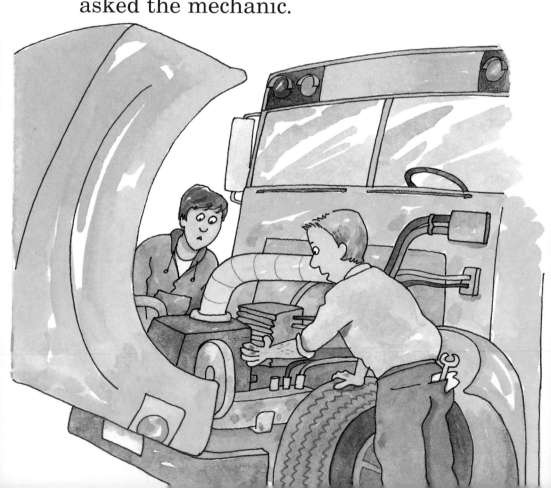

"It went *CA-LUNK!*"
said the bus driver.
She bent way over the engine.
Fluffy fell out of her pocket.
Yowie! he cried.

Fluffy grabbed a rod.

It was oily.

He could not hold on.

He grabbed a cable.

It was greasy.

His paws slipped off.

He grabbed something that
looked like a rope.

Got it! thought Fluffy.

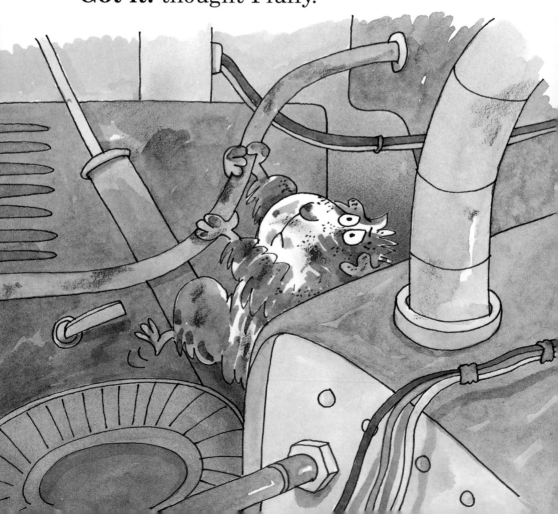

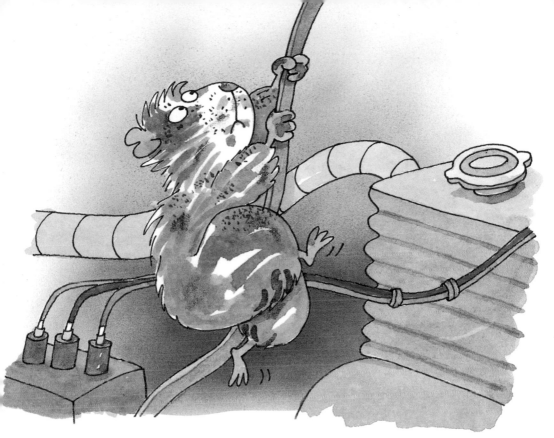

Fluffy held on to that rope.
He pulled himself up, up, up.
At last he poked his head
out of the greasy engine.
Here I am! thought Fluffy.

"The little pig found
a broken fan belt,"
said the mechanic.
"Now I can fix this bus."
The bus driver picked up Fluffy.
"Nice going, little pig!" she said.
It was dirty work, thought Fluffy.
**But somebody had
to do it!**

Fluffy's Pizza Party

The mechanic put in a
new fan belt.
By the time he finished,
it was suppertime.
"Let's order a pizza," he said.

"Good idea,"
said the tow truck driver.
"Yes," said the school bus driver.
"Let's have a pizza party
for the pig."
All right! thought Fluffy.
Party time!

The tow truck driver
phoned for the pizza.
The mechanic
turned on his radio.

Shimmy to the left, now, baby!
Boogie to the right!
Turn around, jump up and down!
Dance all night.

"Can you dance, little pig?"
the school bus driver asked Fluffy.
Who, me? thought Rock Star Fluffy.
He danced up a storm.

"The pizza is here!"
called the tow truck driver.
Everyone hurried
over to the table.
The pizza was topped
with red and green peppers.
Oh, boy! thought Fluffy.
He jumped on his slice
and dug in.

"Time to go, little pig,"
said the school bus driver.
Fluffy waved good-bye
to the tow truck driver
and the mechanic.

Then the bus driver put Fluffy
back into her pocket.
She got into the school bus.
It started right up.

On the ride to Jasmine's house,
Fluffy thought about his lollipop.
He thought about the purple goo
and about being a rock star.
He remembered riding in the tow truck
and how he helped fix the school bus.
He licked some pizza sauce
off his back leg.
What a day! thought Fluffy.
It doesn't get any better than this.

The bus driver rang Jasmine's bell.
"FLUFFY!" Jasmine cried
when she opened the door.
"You poor pig!"
"Oh, he's all right,"
said the school bus driver.
She winked at Fluffy.
"Good-bye, little pig!"

Jasmine took Fluffy inside.
"I'm sorry I forgot you,"
she said. "I will give you
a warm bath. I will feed you
carrots and apples.
I will tuck you into my doll bed
and rock you all night long."
She hugged Fluffy.
"Poor lost pig," she said.
"It must have been awful."

Yeah, thought Fluffy as he snuggled under a warm blanket. **Just awful!**

Fluency Fun

The words in each list below end in the same sounds.
Read the words in a list.
Read them again.
Read them faster.
Try to read all 15 words in one minute.

fight	**bar**	**day**
light	**car**	**gray**
night	**far**	**pray**
right	**jar**	**stay**
bright	**star**	**playing**

Look for these words in *Fluffy's School Bus Adventure*.

would	**thought**	**again**
work	**everyone**	

Note to Parents:

According to *A Dictionary of Reading and Related Terms*, fluency is "the ability to read smoothly, easily, and readily with freedom from word-recognition problems." Fluency is necessary for good comprehension and enjoyable reading. The activities on this page include a speed drill and a sight-recognition drill. Speed drills build fluency because they help students rapidly recognize common syllables and spelling patterns in words, and they're fun! Sight-recognition drills help students smoothly and accurately recognize words. Practice these activities with your child to help him or her become a fluent reader.

—**Wiley Blevins**,
Reading Specialist

For Megan Wirtz, of Washington, D.C.
— K.M.

For Chico and Spike
— M.S.

FLUFFY
GOES TO WASHINGTON

by Kate McMullan
Illustrated by Mavis Smith

President Fluffy?

Fluffy went home with Maxwell
for Presidents' Day weekend.
Maxwell's family drove
to Washington, D.C.,
to visit Maxwell's cousin, Abby.
Fluffy went, too.

Maxwell's sister, Violet, sang
the whole way there:
"Fluffy-wuffy is a pig, E-I-E-I-O!"
It was a long trip.

When Maxwell's family got to
Washington,
Abby and her mom and dad
ran out to the car.
"Welcome!" they said.

"Hi, Maxwell!" said Abby.

"Hi, Violet! Hey, who is this?"

"This is Fluffy," said Maxwell.

Abby picked up Fluffy.

"Eleanor and Franklin will
love you!" she said.

Everybody loves me, thought
Fluffy.

Abby carried Fluffy to her room.

Maxwell carried his food.

Violet carried his treats.

"Fluffy, this is Franklin," said Abby.

She patted a brown gerbil.

"He is named after Franklin Roosevelt.

Roosevelt was president of the United

States more than 50 years ago."

"And this is Eleanor," said Abby.
She patted a honey-colored gerbil.
"She is named after the First Lady,
Eleanor Roosevelt."
Hi, guys, thought Fluffy.

Maxwell gave Fluffy food and water.
Violet gave him treats.
"You will stay here tomorrow
while we go see Washington,"
Maxwell told Fluffy.
No fair! thought Fluffy.
I want to see Washington, too!

The kids ran off to have pizza.
Eleanor and Franklin came
over to Fluffy's cage.
What president are you named after?
asked Eleanor.
Uh . . . said Fluffy.
President Fluffy? he said.

There was no President Fluffy,
said Franklin.
Too bad, said Fluffy.
He liked the sound of it.
President Fluffy!

**There was President
Washington,**
said Eleanor. **And
President Adams.**

And President Jefferson,
said Franklin.
And President Lincoln.

And President Teddy Roosevelt,
said Eleanor. **Don't forget him.**
Eleanor and Franklin went on and on.
They named president after president.

By morning, Fluffy had heard enough.
He climbed on top
of the wheel in his cage.

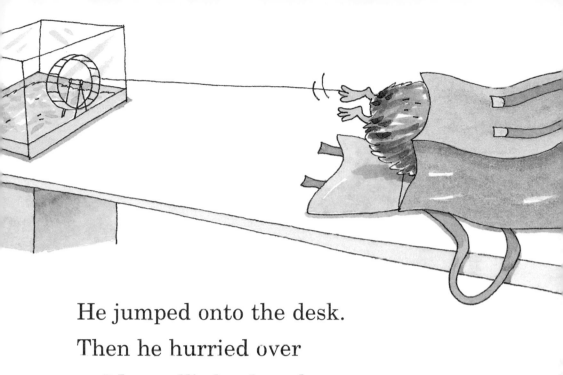

He jumped onto the desk.
Then he hurried over
to Maxwell's backpack
and ran inside.
Look out, Washington! he thought.
Here I come!

Hello, Mr. President

The next morning, Abby took
Maxwell and Violet to the Mall.
"Let's start with the National
Air and Space Museum," she said.

They walked into a big building.

"Wow!" said Maxwell.

"There's the Kitty Hawk Flyer!"

Kitty hawk? thought Fluffy.

That sounded like a very scary animal!

Fluffy peeked out of the backpack.

"Fluffy-wuffy!" said Violet.

Get me out of here, thought Fluffy.

"Fluffy!" said Maxwell. "How did you . . ."

Abby laughed. "I guess he wants to see Washington, too," she said.

I've seen enough! thought Fluffy.

Maxwell held Fluffy up
to see the Kitty Hawk Flyer.
It was not a scary animal.
It was a machine with
two long wings.
"This is the very first airplane," said Abby.
Maxwell showed him Apollo 11.
"That took men to the moon!"
he said.
Cool, thought Fluffy.
Washington isn't so bad.

After a while, Abby said, "Let's go
to the Washington Monument."
They waited in a long line.
At last they got on an elevator.
Fluffy felt himself going up, up, up.
He got a funny feeling in his tummy.

At last they stepped out of the elevator.
"We are in the tallest building
in Washington," said Abby.
Maxwell held Fluffy up
to the window.
Fluffy looked out.
Aaaahhhhh! he thought.
Fluffy shut his eyes.
He did not open them again
until they were back on the ground.

"We have time to see the
Lincoln Memorial," said Abby.
I hope it is not tall, thought Fluffy.
They walked by the Reflecting Pool.
Ducks swam in it.
Hello, duckies! thought Fluffy.

"Here it is," said Abby.

Maxwell held Fluffy up.

"This is President Abraham Lincoln,"
he said.

Fluffy saw a statue of a big man
sitting in a big chair.

Hello, Mr. President, thought Fluffy.

"Abe Lincoln fought a war
to keep our country together,"
said Abby. "He was a great man."

Fluffy looked up at Mr. Lincoln.
So this is a president, he thought.
Fluffy thought he looked very kind.
But he looked worried, too.
Being president must be a hard job,
thought Fluffy.

When they got home, Maxwell
put Fluffy back into his cage.
Where have you been? said
Eleanor.
I've been to see the president,
said Fluffy. **President Abe Lincoln.**
Oh, right, said Franklin.
Fluffy snuggled down in his straw.
If I were named after a president,
he said, **I think I would like
to be called Abe.**

Fluffy at the White House

"Wake up, Fluffy!" said Violet.
"I am going to take you
to the White House! But *shhh!*
It is a secret."
**What's the big deal about
a white house?** thought Fluffy.

You won't get in, Franklin said
as Violet picked Fluffy up.
No, Eleanor said. **They will never
let a pig in the White House!**

Oh, yeah? thought Fluffy.
Well, you don't know this pig!

Violet, Abby, and Maxwell stood
in line for the White House Tour.
Violet kept Fluffy hidden
in her backpack.
He peeked out of a small opening.
But he could not see much.

A man on the lawn had a life-sized
cardboard cutout of the president.
A woman stood next to the cutout.
Snap! The man took her picture.
In the picture, it looked as if the
woman was standing with the president.

"Let's do that!" said Maxwell.

The kids ran over to the man with
the camera.

Violet put down her backpack.

Fluffy peeked out.

He saw a white mouse.

**Take the White Mouse
White House Tour!** the mouse said.

Why not? thought Fluffy.

Fluffy followed the mouse
through a mouse hole
into the White House.
They ran through a tunnel.
They stopped at a small hole.
**Take a peek at the White House
Library,** said the mouse.

Fluffy peeked. He saw a room
with many, many books.
They are all by American writers,
said the mouse.
So many books! thought Fluffy.

The mouse showed Fluffy the
Green Room.
And the Blue Room. And the Red Room.
For a white house, thought Fluffy,
it sure has lots of colors!

Now for the White House Pets!
said the mouse. He showed Fluffy
a picture of a dog named Fala.
And a dog named Millie.
Millie had puppies in the White House,
said the mouse.

The mouse showed Fluffy a picture
of a mockingbird and a raccoon
named Rebecca.
**The pets in the other picture
belonged to President Teddy
Roosevelt,** said the mouse.
Fluffy looked. His eyes grew big.
It was a picture of two guinea pigs.
All right! said Fluffy.
White House pigs!

After one more stop,
the White Mouse White House
Tour ended.
Fluffy popped out of a mouse hole.
At the same time, Maxwell,
Violet, and Abby came out of their
White House Tour.
"Fluffy!" said Maxwell. "How did you . . ."
I'll never tell, thought Fluffy.

Back at Abby's house,
Maxwell put Fluffy into his cage.
Eleanor and Franklin came over.
**You didn't get into the White House,
did you?** said Eleanor.
Yes, I did, said Fluffy.

Oh, right, said Franklin.

I can prove it, said Fluffy.

Oh, right, said Eleanor and Franklin.

Tah-dah! said Fluffy.

Fluffy smiled.

A picture, he thought,

is worth a thousand words.

FLUFFY

LEARNS TO SWIM

FLUFFY
LEARNS TO SWIM

by Kate McMullan
Illustrated by Mavis Smith

Guinea Pigs Don't Swim

Wade's family drove to their lake house.
Wade asked Maxwell to come along.
The boys brought Fluffy, too.

"We can swim in the lake all day,"
said Wade.

"Hot dog!" said Maxwell.

"Can Fluffy go swimming, too?"

"He can't swim," said Wade.

Right! thought Fluffy. **Pigs don't swim.**

Everyone ran into the lake house
to put on a swimsuit.
"Too bad you don't have
a swimsuit, Fluffy," said Wade.
I don't need one, thought Fluffy.
Pigs don't swim.

The boys carried Fluffy's cage
down to the lake.
Wade's Mom was already there.
So was his big sister, Zoe,
and his little sister, Charlotte.
Zoe had some plastic rings.
She slid them onto Charlotte's arms
and blew them up.

"What are those?" asked Maxwell.

"Water wings," said Zoe.

"They help Charlotte keep her head above water. But Charlotte can't go into the lake alone because she can't swim yet."

Just like me, thought Fluffy.

Zoe took Charlotte into the lake.

Wade picked up a yellow water wing.

He looked at the water wing.

He looked at Fluffy.

Don't even think about it,

thought Fluffy.

Wade put Fluffy into the middle
of the water wing.
Maxwell blew it up.
Fluffy felt the ring get tight.
I feel like a hot dog in a bun!
thought Fluffy.

Maxwell stopped blowing and
tucked in the plug.
The boys carried Fluffy into the lake.
"Now you can swim, Fluffy!" Wade said.
One little problem, thought Fluffy.
Pigs don't swim!

The boys put Fluffy in the water.

Fluffy bobbed up and down.

"Go, Fluffy!" said Maxwell and Wade.

Uh-oh! thought Fluffy.

The boys turned toward the shore.

"Zoe! Charlotte! Look!" called Maxwell.

"Fluffy is swimming!" called Wade.

A puff of wind blew Fluffy
across the lake.
When the boys looked back,
Fluffy was far away.

"Oh, no!" said Maxwell.

"Hold on, Fluffy!" called Wade.

"We will save you!"

When? thought Fluffy.

How about NOW?

A dog paddled by.

Nice doggy, thought Fluffy.

A fish leapt out of the lake.

Down, fish! thought Fluffy.

A boat roared by. It made big waves.
The waves bounced Fluffy around.
He was getting dizzy.
Glug! thought Fluffy.
Somebody help this pig!

Just then, a hook caught the water wing.

Fluffy heard a hissing sound.

Air was leaking out!

I am a sinking pig! thought Fluffy.

HELP! HELP! HELP!

Suddenly, something yanked Fluffy
out of the water.
The next thing he knew,
a girl with a fishing pole
was staring at him.
He was swinging
on the end of her fishing line.
Nice catch! thought Fluffy.

The Swimming Lesson

The girl and her father
took Fluffy out of the water wing.
They dried him off with a towel.
"Can I keep him?" said the girl.
"I will call him Fishy."
Fishy? thought Fluffy.
I don't think so.

Just then Wade and Maxwell
ran over.
"That's our guinea pig!" said Wade.
The girl gave Fluffy to him.
"Fluffy!" said Wade. "You're alive!"
"Thank you for saving him,"
Maxwell told the girl.
"Bye, Fishy!" said the girl.

Wade and Maxwell carried Fluffy
back to his cage.
They fed him an apple.
They scratched him behind the ears.
Ahhh! thought Fluffy.
A pig could get used to this.

"That was a close one," said Wade.

"You know what we have to do?"
said Maxwell.

"We have to teach Fluffy to swim."

No way! thought Fluffy.

Wade and Maxwell carried Fluffy back
into the lake.

"This is how I do the crawl," Wade said.

"I put my face in the water.

I blow bubbles through my nose."

Through your *nose*? thought Fluffy.

"Then I move my arms and kick," said Wade.

Fluffy put his face in the water.
He tried to blow bubbles through
his nose.
He tried to move his arms and kick.
But he came up sputtering.

"Fluffy can't do the crawl like we do,"
said Maxwell. "But maybe
he can paddle like a dog."
Maxwell held Fluffy under his tummy.
"Paddle with your paws," he said.
Fluffy paddled.
Now what? he thought.

Maxwell took his hand away.
Fluffy started to sink.
Maxwell picked him up.
"I guess guinea pigs don't swim,"
Wade said.
Right! thought Fluffy.
Pigs don't swim!

Aqua Pig!

The boys put Fluffy down on the dock.

"See you later, Fluffy!" they said.

Then they jumped into the lake and

swam off.

Zoe and her friends came by.
They patted Fluffy and fed him a carrot.
"We are the Aqua Girls," Zoe told Fluffy.
"We are going to be in a big water show.
Watch what we do."

Fluffy watched the Aqua Girls
swim out into the lake.
They turned over onto their backs.
They each put one leg up in the air.
They pointed their toes.
Wow! thought Fluffy.

The Aqua Girls floated on their backs.
They put both feet up in the air.
They reached up with their hands
and touched their toes.
They sank slowly into the lake.
Then they bobbed up again.
Cool, thought Fluffy.

I wish I could be in a big water show,
thought Fluffy. He closed his eyes.
"Most guinea pigs don't swim,"
said the announcer.
"But there is one who does.
Put your hands together
for the one and only . . . Aqua Pig!"

The fans clapped and cheered
as Aqua Pig paddled out into the lake.
He put his face in the water.
He blew bubbles through his nose.
He moved his arms and kicked.
"Yay!" called the fans.

Aqua Pig turned over onto his back.

He put one hind leg up in the air.

He pointed his toes.

"Bravo!" shouted the fans.

Aqua Pig floated on his back.
He put both hind feet up in the air.
He reached up with his front paws
and touched his toes.
Aqua Pig sank slowly into the lake.
"Hooray for Aqua Pig!" yelled the crowd.

Aqua Pig bobbed up again.
He heard the crowd cheering,
"Fluffy! Fluffy! Fluffy!"
Aqua Pig opened his eyes.
"Fluffy! Fluffy!" Wade was saying.
"Wake up. You were dreaming."

The boys took Fluffy back
into the lake.
They put him down
in very shallow water.
Fluffy's paws touched the sand.
Here comes Aqua Pig! thought
Fluffy.

Fluffy kept his head up.

He kept his feet on the sand.

He began to trot through the water.

"Look, Zoe!" called Maxwell.

"Fluffy learned to swim!"

Zoe and the Aqua Girls ran over.

"Is Fluffy doing the crawl?" said Zoe.

"Not really," said Wade.

"Is he doing the dog paddle?" said Zoe.

"Not exactly," said Maxwell.

"Then what *is* he doing?" said Zoe.

I call it the pig paddle, thought Fluffy.

"Just look at him go!" said Wade.